# *Challenge at Second Base*

by Matt Christopher

Illustrated by Marcy Ramsey

Little, Brown and Company
Boston   Toronto   London

First Paperback Edition

The characters and events in this book are fictitious. Any similarity to
real persons, living or dead, is coincidental and not intended by the
author.

ISBN 0-316-14249-2

Library of Congress Catalog Card Number 62-8310
Library of Congress Cataloging-in-Publication information is available.

10 9 8 7 6 5 4 3 2 1

MV NY

Published simultaneously in Canada
by Little, Brown & Company (Canada) Limited

Printed in the United States of America

To Fred and Gloria

*Challenge at Second Base*

## ··· 1

The white runabout hopped and skipped over the rough water like a rabbit chased by a fox. Not far away a bird glided down, touched the water with its bill, and swooped away.

Stan, sitting on the rear seat behind his brother Phil, felt the bumps. Suddenly his eyes opened wide and he straightened as if somebody had prodded him in the back.

Wasn't this Monday? The day the baseball suits were given out?

Stan's heart flipped. Yes, it was!

"Look at me!" he cried out loud. "Playing around in the middle of Lake Mohawk! Phil!"

he yelled into the wind to the boat's pilot. "Phil, what time is it?"

Phil looked at his wrist watch. "Five minutes of five!" he answered over his shoulder.

"Holy catfish!" shouted Stan. "They were passing out the suits at four-thirty! I have to get home and get out of my trunks, Phil!"

"You won't right away!" replied Phil. "Look ahead of us and to our left! Somebody's in trouble!"

"But, Phil!" Stan protested. "I've got to —"

"Not till we help out that guy first!" said Phil sternly.

Stan squinted past the sharp bow of the boat, to the left of Phil's head. He saw something white in the water, but could not make out what it was. He stood up, angry at himself for having let the time go by unnoticed.

"It's a sailboat!" he yelled. "Somebody's waving at us!"

The sailboat was lying on its side, its white

4

sail flapping in the water. A person was clinging to it, waving frantically.

Phil gunned the motor and turned the wheel. A short scream burst from Stan as he lost his balance and started to fall. For a brief moment he was looking straight down at the deep green water. His face was hardly more than two feet away from it. Then his hands gripped the edge of the boat and he held on tightly.

Seconds later he was sitting down, his heart pounding.

Quickly, Phil approached the tipped sailboat. He cut the motor and the boat lost speed.

Stan was able to read the name on the boat, even though it was upside down. *Mary Lou*.

"It's Jeb Newman's boat!" Stan cried. "That's Jeb!"

"Hi, guys!" greeted the boy in the water. He was grinning as if a tipped sailboat were

5

a common occurrence with him. "Thanks for the rescue!"

"We'll help you put her back up!" said Phil.

Jeb was wearing swim trunks. Stan expected to see Gary with him. Gary was Jeb's younger brother, a strong prospect for second base on the Falcons' team. That was all right, except that Stan wanted to play second base, too.

Phil let the motor idle as he drifted close to the sailboat. Stan dived in, and he and Jeb swam to the other side of the boat. While Phil lifted the mast, Stan and Jeb pushed against the side of the boat until it was back up in position.

Jeb climbed into it, the water inside the boat up to his shins. Then Phil helped pull Stan back into the motorboat.

"A gust of wind caught me off my guard while I was turning," explained Jeb. "Guess

I'm still an amateur." He unhooked a pail and began bailing out the water.

"How come you're not at the ball park?" he asked Stan. "You're playing with the Falcons, aren't you?"

"I forgot about it," said Stan, and looked anxiously at his brother. "Maybe we can still make it, Phil."

"See you around, Jeb!" yelled Phil, and once more gunned the motor.

The sudden burst of noise frightened a flock of birds flying low near them. Stan was afraid he had little chance beating out Gary at second base. After all, why shouldn't Gary be good? Jeb was working him out a lot — going to the field with him when nobody else was there and hitting grounders to him for hours.

If Phil would help Stan like that, Stan would be good, too. Phil, though, acted as if he didn't care whether Stan played or not.

Stan shook his head. He just couldn't fig-

7

ure out Phil anymore. Last year Phil had played professional baseball with Harport. This year he didn't play at all, except pitch and catch with Stan. And Stan practically would have to twist his arm to get him to do that.

"I'm afraid we'll be late, Stan," said Phil.

"I'm afraid, too," replied Stan sadly.

# ··· 2

Phil drove Stan directly to the baseball field. The place was as empty as an open sea.

"Guess I don't get a suit." Stan's voice caught a little.

"Don't lose all your hopes," replied Phil. "The coach is probably holding one for you."

"I doubt it," said Stan. "Coach Bartlett is real strict about these things. He said that if a boy didn't have a good reason for not showing up at practice, he wasn't interested in playing. He was keeping out somebody else who was."

"But you have a good reason for not being

9

here this afternoon," said Phil. "It was my fault."

Stan didn't answer.

On the way home in the car, Stan got to thinking about Phil. From the brief conversation he had between Mom and Dad, he knew that Phil hadn't done too well with Harport. Even so, he could have signed a contract with them this year, but he had refused. Stan didn't know exactly why Phil had refused. If Stan were in that position he certainly would not have!

"Why didn't you play with Harport this year, Phil?" Stan asked. "Did you want more money?"

"What?" Phil seemed to be daydreaming. "Oh! No. No, it wasn't money," he said finally.

"Then what was it?"

Phil looked at Stan. He seemed a little embarrassed. "You won't mind if I don't want to talk about it, will you, little buddy?"

Stan shrugged. "No. If you don't want to."

He couldn't understand it at all. What other reason was it if it wasn't money?

Well, Stan had his own worries now. Without a suit he couldn't play for the Falcons in the league. What was he going to do now? Most of his pals would make the team. He was sure of that.

I'll have more time with my space projects, he told himself. I don't have to play baseball. But he was just thinking up excuses, for he loved baseball more than anything.

Saturday afternoon, Larry Jones and Tommy Hart came to the house, dressed in brand-new baseball uniforms. They were carrying their spikes and gloves. Larry's was a catcher's mitt.

"Where were you yesterday afternoon?" Larry asked. He was almost as wide as he was tall. His hair was copper-colored, and he had freckles sprinkled around his nose.

11

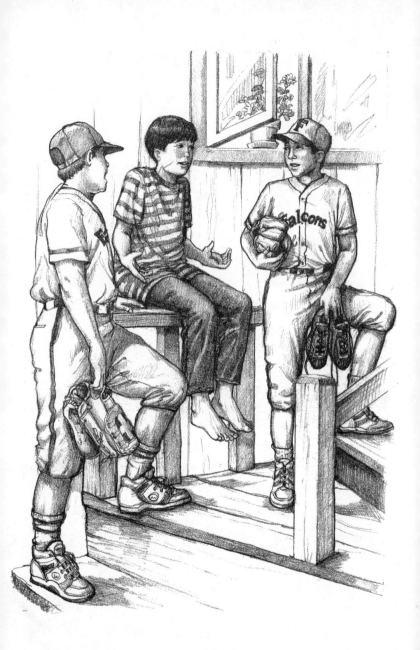

"Didn't you know Coach Bartlett was passing out the suits?"

"I got there too late," said Stan.

"You should've been there," said Tommy. "You would've gotten a suit." He was the team's pitcher, a tall, slender boy who could hit as well as he could throw.

"Was Gary there?" Stan asked quickly.

"Of course," replied Tommy. "You don't think he'd miss it, do you?"

"We're going down to the field, now," said Larry. "Jeb Newman is going to pick us up here."

"Here?" Stan frowned. "Why here?"

Larry shrugged his large shoulders. "Because we told him to. You're coming along, aren't you?"

"I don't have a suit," said Stan. "If Coach Bartlett had wanted to give me one, he would have brought it over by now — I guess."

"Our first league game is Monday," Tommy said. "Against the Jaguars."

13

Why are they telling me this? thought Stan. I don't want to hear it!

Just then Jeb Newman drove his car up to the curb. Beside him sat his brother Gary in baseball cap and uniform.

Larry and Tommy trotted to the car and got in.

"Aren't you coming?" Gary called.

Stan shook his head, turned, and went back into the house.

Outside, the car roared away from the curb.

# ··· 3

Three shelves lined one of the walls in Stan's room. His Dad had built them for him, and painted them blue. Half of the lowest shelf contained books. All kinds of books — adventure, science fiction, and sports.

The remainder of the shelf, and the other two, contained a variety of models. Airplanes, ships, submarines, rockets, and satellites. In one corner stood a table about four feet square. On it was a miniature space base similar to that of Cape Canaveral. Every piece had been put together and glued by Stan's own hands.

Right now Stan was assembling a spacestation model. This he was going to suspend by a string from the ceiling to give the illusion of a real space station in outer space.

"Stan!" It was Mom. "You have a friend here to see you!"

"Okay!" he answered. "Send him in!"

He couldn't leave his model now, not while he was holding two parts of it together, waiting for the glue to dry.

In a moment Tommy Hart came in. His face broadened in a smile as he looked at the many models that decorated the room.

"Boy!" he said. "Would I like something like this!"

Stan grinned with pride. "They were kits. Dad bought most of them for me. Others I got for doing odd jobs."

Tommy took a few moments gazing wonder-eyed at the models, then came and stood beside Stan. "We lost to the Jaguars Monday," he said unhappily. "Four to one."

"Who pitched?" asked Stan.

"I did. Did we look bad! Don missed two

16

at short, and Duffy misjudged a fly in center field with a man on."

He began telling about other incidents that resulted in their losing the game. Stan just listened. He wasn't interested in hearing a play-by-play description of the game, but he wouldn't tell Tommy that. He liked Tommy, and he wouldn't say anything to Tommy that might hurt him.

Mom's voice carried to him again from the kitchen. "Somebody else to see you, Stanley!"

By now the glue was dry. Stan left the partially completed space station on the bench and looked behind Tommy. The overweight catcher of the Falcons came strolling into the room, shouldering a baseball bat. Sporting a mischievous smile, he stopped in the middle of the room and stood admiring Stan's models.

"You going to be an astronaut?" he asked Stan.

"I'd like to," replied Stan.

"Me, too. But I don't think they'll make a space ship big enough to hold me," said Larry.

He walked up close to the table on which stood the space-base model.

"Gary Newman looked great on second," he said over his shoulder. "He didn't make an error and he hit the ball every time."

"Sure," said Tommy. "And always into somebody's hands."

"That's better than not hitting the ball at all," replied Larry. "I struck out once, and you did, too." He looked around at Stan. "Why didn't you come to the game, Stan?"

Stan colored. "Why should I? I didn't get a suit."

"You weren't there. You might have gotten one if you were there. You know what the guys are saying?"

"Larry," Tommy broke in. "Don't you think you're talking too much?"

Stan looked at Tommy and back at Larry.

"What are you guys trying to say?" he asked suspiciously.

Larry shrugged. "They're saying you didn't want to show up when the suits were given out because you were afraid you wouldn't get one!"

Stan swallowed. He got out of his chair quickly and faced Larry. "I wanted to go, but I couldn't get there! I was in a boat!"

"I know," said Larry in a softer voice. "We heard about it."

Stan frowned. So that was it. They had figured that would be the excuse I'd give for not being at the ball park.

His eyes narrowed. "You figured the same as they did, didn't you, Larry? You figured that I —"

"Oh, no, Stan! Not me! Honest!"

Larry's face reddened, and he backed away a little.

"Watch it, Larry!" yelled Tommy.

But it was too late. The top of Larry's bat

struck one of the rocket models standing on the top shelf. It fell to the floor and broke into a dozen pieces!

Stan stared at the pieces, then at Larry. Hurt choked him. Then anger rose so quickly in him he began shouting before he thought.

"You fat, clumsy ox! Look what you did! Why did you have to bring that lousy bat in here? Why —"

Larry stared at him, his face paling. Then he stooped and picked up the pieces of broken rocket model. His chubby hands were trembling.

"I'll pay for it," he murmured. "Tell me how much it was."

"I can't remember," snapped Stan.

Larry put the pieces on the bench beside the space-ship model Stan was working on, and walked to the door.

Suddenly he turned around. His face was beet red.

"I'm glad you're not on our team, Stan

Martin!" he cried angrily. "You know that? I'm real glad! You're just like your brother! Everybody knows he wasn't good either!"

The words fell on Stan like hailstones. He wanted to say something, but couldn't.

Larry left hastily, and Tommy, looking embarrassed, followed him out.

Hardly had they left when Phil came into the room. Surely he must have heard Larry's unkind and untrue remarks. But, if he had, he didn't show it.

"I have a couple of things here for you, little buddy," he said, a warm smile on his lips.

He handed Stan an envelope. Whatever the other thing was he held behind his back, out of Stan's sight.

Stan stared at the envelope. It was very strange. His name and address were made up of words cut out from a newspaper and pasted on the envelope!

He ripped open the end of it and pulled

out the letter. This, too, was written with words cut out from a newspaper. Stan read the letter and sucked in his breath.

DON'T QUIT! YOU HAVE ABILITY! STICK TO IT!

It wasn't signed.

## ··· 4

P hil!" Stan cried. "Read this! Who would
send me a letter like this?"

Phil read the letter and whistled. "How
do you like that?" he said. "Somebody's interested in you, little buddy, and wants to
keep it a secret!"

"But why?"

Phil shrugged. "I don't know. Whoever it
is must like you, that's for sure." He handed
the letter back to Stan. "Well, that should
be enough surprise for one day, but here's
another."

He brought his other hand around from
behind him, and gave Stan a gray box. Al-

most instantly Stan knew what was in it. He took it and opened it.

"My baseball suit!" he shouted.

He lifted the jersey out of the box, held it against himself for size, then looked at the number 10 sewn on the back.

"Saw Mr. Bartlett on the street," explained Phil. "He told me to give this to you, and for you to be at practice tonight at five."

After his excitement wore off a little, Stan telephoned Tommy Hart and told him the good news.

"See? Didn't I tell you?" cried Tommy. "Going to practice tonight?"

"I have a suit, haven't I?" replied Stan.

"I'll meet you in front of your house," said Tommy.

He was at Stan's house at a quarter of five. The two of them walked to the field, carrying their gloves and spikes. Stan felt as if he were dreaming. Was Coach Bartlett actually

choosing him over Gary Newman, or had the coach only picked him to warm the bench?

Some of the players were already at the field playing catch. However, there was one player in the infield working on grounders. It was Gary Newman. And hitting a ball to him was his brother Jeb.

"He really wants to make sure he plays, doesn't he?" said Tommy, a trace of disgust in his voice.

"He probably will, too," replied Stan. To himself he thought, *I wish somebody would work me out like that.*

Soon a car pulled up to the curb, stopped, and a tall, thin man wearing a T-shirt stepped out. From the trunk of the car he dragged out a huge, dirt-smudged bag and carried it toward the dugout. He spotted Stan and grinned.

"Hi, Stan! We missed you!"

Stan smiled bashfully.

Jeb quit hitting to Gary and retired to the

dugout to watch. Coach Bartlett put the boys through batting practice first, with Larry behind the plate and George Page throwing. Stan tried to avoid Larry as much as possible. When he batted he didn't speak, nor did Larry.

A left-hand hitter, Stan socked a couple of grounders, missed a pitch, and blasted a fly to right field.

After batting practice the coach asked Jeb to hit fly balls to the outfielders.

"Stan, alternate with Gary at second," he said.

It was as Stan had expected. Most of the other infielders had their positions pretty well cinched: Larry behind the plate; George Page at first; Jim Kendall at third; and Don Marion at short. They were a year or two older than Stan and Gary, more experienced and better ballplayers. It was at second base that the team was weakest.

Coach Bartlett knocked grounders to his

infielders till the sweat rolled down their faces and they showed signs of tiredness. Stan missed several. The coach would then hit him high bounders, with "handles" on them, which Stan gloved easily. But Gary had no trouble. He was fielding the grounders skillfully, and pegging them accurately to first.

"Okay, that's it," said the coach finally. "Bring it in."

Jeb helped the coach put the balls and equipment back into the big canvas bag. Stan, carrying a bat toward them, heard them talking, and hesitated a moment. Distinctly, he heard the coach say:

"He's going to be a real ballplayer. Watch him in two or three years."

"He loves it," said Jeb.

"Loves it? I've never seen a kid with so much interest and desire. Believe me, that kid's a natural!"

Stan knew they were talking about Gary.

28

Silently, he laid the bat down and walked away.

# ··· 5

The line-up for the Falcons in the game against the Steelers was as follows:

| | |
|---|---|
| D. Marion | shortstop |
| J. Kendall | third base |
| F. Smith | left field |
| D. Powers | center field |
| G. Page | first base |
| G. Newman | second base |
| L. Jones | catcher |
| E. Lee | right field |
| T. Hart | pitcher |

The Falcons, taking their first raps, got two runs in the first inning to start them off. The Steelers' pitcher, a small, broad-shouldered boy with hair that needed cutting, allowed a walk and two hits. One of them was a triple off the powerful bat of Bert "Duffy" Powers. Duffy, a tall, quiet boy with glasses, couldn't make it home, for George struck out and Gary popped to short.

The Steelers managed to put a man on first, but there he stayed. Tommy's straight ball was cutting the corners, and the umpire was calling them as he saw them.

Larry, leading off in the second inning, belted a long fly to center. The soaring meteor drew a quick response from the fans, but before the chubby catcher got halfway to first, the fielder caught the ball for the out.

Then Eddie Lee hit a zigzagging grounder to the pitcher. The pitcher fumbled it, and for a moment it looked as if Eddie might get on. But then the husky pitcher closed his hand on the ball, reared back, and heaved it to first. Eddie was out by half a step.

Tommy Hart waited for the one he

wanted. With a two-two count on him he belted a single between short and third.

Stan, sitting in the shade of the dugout, looked across at Mr. Bartlett standing in the third-base coaching box. Would the coach give Tommy the steal signal? Tommy was fast, but he was pitching and there were two outs. Stan waited anxiously to see what the coach would do.

The coach gave no signal, which meant for lead-off man Don Marion to hit away.

Don socked the second pitch high over second base. The shortstop and the second baseman both ran for it, but the Steelers' other outfielders yelled, "Barry! Barry!" The second baseman made the catch. Three outs.

Again the Steelers failed to score.

In the top of the third the Falcons put across three more runs, and in the fourth two more. It looked like a runaway for them.

Meanwhile, three grounders had zipped down to Gary at second, and he had fielded them all. Stan wondered if Coach Bartlett would put him in the game. He wouldn't mind playing now, especially since the Falcons were far in the lead.

In the bottom of the fourth inning his wish was granted. He replaced Gary at second. A high-bouncing grounder came to him, and for a moment a frightening sensation came over him. What if he muffed this one?

The next instant the ball struck the pocket of his glove. He yanked it out and snapped it to first.

"Out!" shouted the umpire.

The wave of fright left him. That, thought Stan, wasn't bad at all.

The next two men failed to reach first either.

With two outs in the fifth, Ronnie Woods, a left-hand hitter, pinch-hit for Frankie Smith. He looked awfully dangerous. But he missed two pitches, then popped to first to end the inning.

The Steelers went to the plate with determination. But Tommy, pitching one-hit ball so far, didn't let a man get to first.

Duffy led off in the sixth. Standing eagerly at the plate, waving his bat gently, he looked threatening. The first pitch came in and he swung.

*Crack!* It went sailing far out to left field! It cleared the fence by twenty feet!

But it was no homer. It was foul by ten feet.

"Straighten this one out, Duffy!" the boys on the bench yelled.

Blast! Another terrific poke out to left! But again it went foul.

Then Duffy let the third pitch go by.

"You're out!" cried the umpire.

Duffy whirled, stared at the man, then went sulking to the dugout.

"That blind bat," muttered Duffy. "It was way outside."

"George Page, then Stan Martin," said the scorekeeper. "Get on deck, Stan."

George walked to the plate, a bat on his

shoulder. Stan selected one from the dozen on the ground and swung it back and forth a few times. Then he knelt in the on-deck circle waiting for his turn. It came quickly. George popped the first pitch to third for the second out.

Stan stood nervously at the plate, batting left-handed.

"Wait for a good one!" he heard Coach Bartlett say.

The pitch came in chest-high. It was beautiful. It was the kind of pitch he liked. But he didn't swing.

"Strike one!"

Another pitch came in. Lower now, but not too low. He swung. *Crack!* A grounder down the first-base line. He started to run. The ball went foul halfway to first, and Stan went back to the plate.

"Ball!" An outside pitch.

"One and two!" said the umpire, announcing the count.

The next pitch came down the groove. Stan belted it. A line drive over the first baseman's head! Stan dropped the bat and raced to first.

He had done it. His first time at bat, and he had singled. He heard the praises from the fans, and he heard it from Coach Bartlett.

"Nice hit, Stanley, boy!"

What now? A steal? Would the coach have him try it with two outs?

The coach slipped his thumbs behind his belt. That didn't mean anything.

Larry took the first pitch. It was a ball.

The coach still had his thumbs behind his belt. Now he moved his hands along the belt to his hips. This meant something. The steal was on!

Stan waited till the pitcher climbed the mound, then took a safe lead off the bag. The pitcher lifted his arms, brought them down, looked over his shoulder at first, then threw home.

"Strike!" said the umpire.

Stan took off, his spikes pounding the ground, leaving puffs of dust behind him.

He slid into second. Dust clouded around him. The second baseman caught the peg from his catcher and slapped it on Stan. But Stan was already there.

Two outs, Stan on second, and the count on Larry was one ball, one strike. The stocky catcher dug in on the first pitch, and whacked it far out to deep center! He had hit one like this in the second inning.

The Steelers' center fielder turned around and bolted back. He was nearly against the center-field fence when he lifted his glove. The ball plopped into it and stuck there.

The fans groaned. This time Larry managed to get a little closer to first than he did before.

"Tough luck, Larry!" The boys on the bench echoed his feelings. "You'll get it over that fence yet!"

Stan had started running at the crack of the bat. Now, crossing home plate, he stopped a moment and smiled at the unlucky catcher.

"He played for you, Larry, or it would've been a hit," he said.

Larry paused, his eyes meeting Stan's for a moment while both of them thought back to that embarrassing incident in Stan's room when Larry, hurt from the shameful words Stan had called him, shouted an outburst back at Stan. Afterwards Stan had been sorry for what he'd said.

Suddenly a grin spread across Larry's sweating face.

"Thanks, Stan," he said.

And right away you could tell he had been sorry, too.

## ··· 6

The lead-off man for the Steelers walked, then raced to second base on a scratch hit to third. Jim Kendall charged the ball, but by the time he fielded it and snapped it to second, the runner was there.

"Let's get a double, Stan!" Don shouted from short.

A right-hander was batting. Although it was the bottom of the sixth inning and the Falcons were leading, 7 to 0, Stan felt nervous. A double play would mean two outs and only one more to get to complete the inning. Three more on top of that would complete the game.

But if he goofed on the play, the Steelers could start a rally. There were many games — even in the major leagues — when a losing team scored several runs in the closing innings of a game to win it.

Tommy got his signal from Larry and put his foot on the rubber. He took his stretch, checked the runners on first and second, then threw.

*Crack!* A sizzling grounder to short!

Stan ran to cover second. Don fielded the ball and snapped it to him. Nervously, Stan caught it. At the same time he feared the runner's bumping into him before he could throw the ball.

In one motion he turned his body to first and threw. Horror overwhelmed him as he saw his throw going too wide for George to catch. The ball just missed the runner, and went bouncing toward the fence.

There was his chance to pull off a good

play, and he had muffed it. Gary would have thrown it perfectly. *I bet right now he's laughing up his sleeve.*

Now it was one out and men on second and third.

Tommy worked hard on the batter. With two strikes and a ball on him, the hitter blasted a line drive to third. The ball traveled like a white bullet about seven feet off the ground. Jim lifted his hands. *Smack!* The ball struck his glove. But then it went through and fell to the ground!

The runner on third rushed back to tag up. Now, realizing that Jim had missed the hard-driven ball, he turned and streaked for home.

"Home, Jim! Home!" Don Marion shouted.

Jim picked up the ball and pegged it home. Larry, straddling the plate, caught the ball coming in like an arrow. He put it on the sliding runner, and the umpire jerked up his thumb.

"Out!"

Two outs, men on first and second. They hadn't tried to advance on the play.

The Steelers' next hitter waited out the pitches. Then, with a three-two count on him, he cut at a knee-high pitch. Whiff! Another strike-out for Tommy.

Coach Bartlett put in pinch-hitters in the top of the seventh, but nobody hit. The Steelers took their turn at bat for the last time in the game. Three men up, three men down. They lost, 7 to 0.

Stan didn't linger around to listen to the comments about the game. He saw Gary Newman's face and that was enough.


That evening Dottie, Stan's seventeen-year-old sister, got dressed to go out. It was a common routine, and Stan hardly thought about it.

When the front doorbell rang, Stan went to answer it. He found Jeb Newman standing there, and stared.

Jeb taking Dottie out? What was the matter with her head?

"Hi, Stan." Jeb greeted him with a smile. "Dottie, in?"

*You know doggone well she's in,* Stan thought. "Yes, she's in. Just a minute. Hey, Dottie!"

He hardly turned around, though, before she was there, smiling very politely and looking too pretty for a guy like Jeb Newman.

After they left, Stan closed the door disgustedly and turned on the television set in the living room. He watched the program with mild interest, for his mind was on the game he had played today.

Phil came home, wearing gray slacks and a fancy sport shirt.

He smiled at Stan. "Hi, little buddy. How'd you make out?"

"We won," Stan said. "Seven to nothing."

"Wow! Did you play?"

"A few innings."

"Any hits?"

"Singled." Stan paused. "I muffed on a double play."

Phil looked at him. His smile faded.

"Don Marion caught the ground ball and we got the man out at second. But I threw wild to first."

"They didn't get any runs, so what are you worried about?"

"They almost did, though, if Jim Kendall hadn't thrown a man out at home. He missed a line drive, but picked it up in time."

Phil pulled a hassock in front of Stan and sat on it. He placed his hands on Stan's knees and looked at his brother with a warm, kind light in his eyes.

"Little buddy," he said, "you're like me.

You get hurt easily, just the way I do. And neither one of us can help it. Tell me, how much do you like baseball?"

"I like it," Stan said. "I guess I like it better than football or basketball, even."

"It's a tough game," Phil said. "Sometimes you play your heart out, and you'll still fail. You'll sit back and wonder why you've failed. Why didn't you get that hit? Why didn't you catch that ball? Those things will run through your mind and sometimes you'll wish you had never started playing the game."

Stan stared at his brother. "Is that why you're not playing now, Phil?"

Phil shrugged, and avoiding Stan's eyes. "I did all right for a while. Then I missed a few grounders, and at the plate I'd either strike out or hit into somebody's hands. Couldn't do a thing right, so I was benched."

"Didn't they give you another chance?"

"Yes. But I was no longer a regular. I was

afraid that they were going to send me to a team in a lower league, and I didn't want that."

"So you didn't go back at all."

"That's right," said Phil.

"But it's different with you, Phil," said Stan. "You were playing professional."

"At one time I was your age and playing sand-lot ball too," replied Phil.

"But that letter I got," said Stan. "That letter printed from words cut out of a newspaper. It says I shouldn't quit. Who wouldn't want me to quit, Phil?"

Phil grinned and shook his head. "I don't know, little buddy," he said. "Obviously, somebody."

Stan held the *Courier-Star* open to the sports pages, and was reading the Falcons' box score of the game with the Steelers.

|            | AB | H | RBI | R |
|------------|----|---|-----|---|
| Marion ss  | 2  | 1 | 0   | 2 |
| eFinn      | 1  | 0 | 0   | 0 |
| Kendall 3b | 5  | 2 | 0   | 1 |
| Smith lf   | 3  | 2 | 0   | 2 |
| aWoods lf  | 1  | 0 | 0   | 0 |
| Powers cf  | 3  | 2 | 4   | 1 |
| Page lf    | 4  | 0 | 0   | 0 |
| Newman 2b  | 3  | 2 | 0   | 1 |
| bMartin 2b | 1  | 1 | 0   | 0 |
| Jones c    | 3  | 1 | 3   | 0 |
| Lee rf     | 3  | 1 | 0   | 0 |

| | | | |
|---|---|---|---|
| cCollins | 1 | 0 | 0 | 0 |
| Hart p | 3 | 1 | 0 | 0 |
| dR. Jones | 1 | 0 | 0 | 0 |
| Totals | 34 | 13 | 7 | 7 |

a — Flied out for Smith in 5th; b — Singled for Newman in 6th; c — Struck out for Lee in 7th, d — Grounded out for Hart in 7th; e — Popped out for Marion in 7th.

Falcons . . . 203 200 0 — 7
Steelers . . . 000 000 0 — 0

Presently he sensed somebody watching him. He lowered the newspaper and saw Dottie standing behind him with her hands on her hips and a flattering smile on her lips.

"Bet I know what you're reading," she said.

He grinned, and looked back at the paper. "Maybe you do," he answered.

"Oh, don't be so rude," said Dottie. "You got a hit, and you guys won, didn't you? What more do you want?"

"Nothing," he said. He recalled that she had gone out with Jeb Newman the other night, and he went cold all over.

"Why did you go out with that Jeb Newman guy?" he said, talking through the paper. "What's the matter with Joe Warner? Or Tom Miller? You've been out with them before."

"There's nothing wrong with them," she said. "But Jeb's nice, too." She laughed. "You're just prejudiced."

He stared at her over the edge of the paper. "Preju-what?"

"Prejudiced. You don't like him because his brother Gary is working hard to be the regular second baseman on the team, and you want to play second base yourself."

He closed the paper hard, folded it, and tossed it on the coffee table.

"He tells you everything, doesn't he?" Stan said, and started to walk past his sister on his way out of the room.

She grabbed his arm. "Stan," she said, "don't be like that. Jeb is really a nice guy."

He looked up into her green eyes. There was a gentleness in them that brought a smile to his lips.

"Maybe you're right," he said. "Maybe I am preju — whatever that word is."

"Prejudiced." She laughed.

"Maybe I am prejudiced." He echoed her laughter, then turned, and walked out.

The Falcons practiced at five-thirty that afternoon. Jeb was hitting grounders to Gary when the rest of them arrived at the field. *Boy!* Stan thought. *Gary really wants to make sure he plays!*

Coach Bartlett had the boys bat around twice — hitting five and laying one down. Then he showed them how to bunt. Stan watched with strong interest. He had always thought that bunting was just for somebody who couldn't hit. But now he heard the coach explain how really important it was.

51

"A good bunt can advance a man from first to second," he said, "and put that man in a position to score. If a man is on third the batter can squeeze him in. A lot of games have been won with a run squeezed in, so don't take bunting lightly."

On Friday they played the Jaguars. Gary started at second. In the first two innings he handled three grounders without an error. The Jaguars played good defensive ball and began hitting Lefty Kellar hard. The score was tied in the fifth, 3-all. With one out and men on first and third, Coach Bartlett put Tommy Hart in to pitch.

A hit meant at least one run. An extra-base drive could mean two runs.

Tommy threw in some warm-up pitches, then waited for the hitter to enter the batting box. Tension mounted and the infielders began chattering in what sounded like a lot of jumbled words.

"Getimout, Tommy! Getimout!"

"Throweminthere, Tom! Strikeimout!"

Tommy stepped on the rubber, stretched, and delivered. *Crack!* The ball zipped across the infield close to second base. Gary ran hard, reached for the hop, caught it, and snapped the ball to shortstop Don Marion covering the bag. Don whipped the ball to first.

In time! A double play!

"Nice play, Gary," said the coach, as the second baseman came trotting in. "Fielded that ball like a major leaguer. Nice play, Don."

Then the Falcons broke the tie. With a man on first, Duffy Powers socked a double and George Page singled. The Falcons went ahead by two runs.

Stan replaced Gary at second. He snagged a pop fly, then bobbled a grounder. He picked up the ball quickly and, almost without looking, snapped the ball to first. The ball went wide, and the runner advanced to second.

However, the Jaguars didn't score. Neither did they push across any runs in the final inning, and the score ended with the Falcons coming out on top, 5 to 3.

On July 5, Stan played the first three innings and bobbled two grounders. One of them resulted in a run for the opponents, the Red Devils. But the Falcons managed to keep ahead from the first inning on and won again, 3 to 1.

*We're lucky to win,* thought Stan. *I'm playing as if I'm a real rookie!*

He was worried out there. He was thinking about how much better Gary Newman was than he. That was why he kept bobbling so many grounders.

Phil was right. You can love the game with all your heart. But your heart can get hurt awfully easy.

The same thing was happening to Stan that had happened to Phil.

# ··· *8*

The hot July days skipped by quickly. Stan almost forgot about the mysterious letter he had received. He had thought that some member of his family had sent it — perhaps his Dad — but he wasn't·sure.

So far Phil hadn't seen the Falcons play. Stan didn't encourage him, either. Dad and Mom went as often as they could, and so did Dottie.

"I don't see what you're worried about," said Dad after the Falcons' game with the Clippers. "You got a hit and made two assists. Is that bad?"

It did not happen to be bad that time, but the Falcons had lost the game, 7 to 4. Then the Comets gave them a lacing, 6 to 2, a game in which Stan went without a hit. However, he didn't feel so bad. Some of the others went hitless, too, including Duffy Powers.

One warm afternoon, as they were riding in Phil's boat, Larry remarked to Stan and Tommy, "You know, there's one guy who surprises me on our ball team."

"Who?" said Stan.

They were discussing baseball, trying to figure out why the Falcons had lost their third game in a row yesterday. In that game they had gone two extra innings. Then a triple broke the tie, ending the game in the Red Devils' favor, 7 to 6.

"Gary Newman," said Larry. "That guy's really gone to town. Know what his batting average is?"

Stan turned away and looked at the waves swirling alongside the fast-moving boat. He knew, all right. And so did everybody else on the team.

"Three-seventy-two," said Tommy. "The highest on the team."

"And he hasn't missed many at second," went on Larry.

Maybe he didn't realize he was "rubbing it in" Stan. And maybe he did. It was a wonder Stan wasn't benched for good.

The boys had played catch on shore and had brought their gloves and a ball on board with them. Now Stan struck the dark, oily pocket of his fielder's glove hard with his right fist. Why did the guys keep bringing up Gary's name? He wished he had never heard of Gary Newman.

"Hey, you guys!" yelled Phil suddenly. "Look what's coming over that hill at our left!"

The three boys turned. A yell burst from all three. The northwestern sky was almost black. Mountainous clouds bore toward them, twisting in the sky before a strong wind.

A streak of lightning flashed and then thunder rumbled.

"We'd better head for shore right now!" Phil said, turning the wheel of the craft. "Put on your life jackets! We can't take any chances!"

The boys each turned to pick up a life jacket. As Stan reached for his, the boat turned and he lost his balance. Quickly, he caught himself, but his fielder's glove slipped from his hand and went over the edge.

"My glove!" he shouted. "Phil! My glove!"

Panic overtook him as he saw his almost-new glove riding the crest of a wave, then gradually sinking.

If he didn't do something right now, that glove would be gone forever!

Stan dived into the water and felt the pleasant shock of its warmth cover his body. He opened his eyes and looked around hastily. Then he rose, whipped the water from his head and leaped high to look for the glove. Again and again he leaped, searching the dark, greenish water.

Then he knew that the worst had happened. He'd never see that glove again.

# ... *9*

"Y ou crazy fool!" yelled Phil as he slowed the boat alongside Stan so that Tommy and Larry could haul the boy in. "What're you trying to do? Drown?"

"I wanted to save my glove," Stan murmured hoarsely.

"Save your glove?" Larry echoed. "You make it sound as if it was human."

With his friends' help, Stan got into the boat and sat on the rear seat. Instantly, Phil increased the throttle, and the boat began speeding forward again.

"To blazes with the glove!" yelled Phil over his shoulder. "I'm trying to save us from being hit by a storm and you want to save a glove! Try to top that, will you?"

Phil would say that, of course. Perhaps he had never felt the way Stan did about a glove. Perhaps that was why he didn't care about playing baseball any more.

"Here, put this on," said Tommy, and helped Stan with a life jacket.

Stan steadied himself against the bouncing of the boat. Already the waves were rolling high. Drops of water fell upon them. For a moment Stan wasn't sure whether they came from the water about them or the heavy clouds swirling overhead.

Again lightening pierced the sky for a moment and then abruptly vanished. Again thunder rumbled.

The boys hung on for dear life to the sides of the boat. Ahead of them the shoreline seemed to be rising and falling. Trees leaned under the power of the wind. Leaves broke loose from their branches, flew swiftly and crazily through the air. Birds swooped low and high, carried every which way by the wind. The drops fell thicker, and now Stan knew they were falling from those black clouds.

The boat lifted on the crest of a wave, then came down *smack!* The bow pierced the water, and gallons of the churning whiteness spilled into the boat, covering the boys' feet.

Phil hung desperately onto the wheel to keep the boat from getting out of his control. It was up to him now. It was a fight between him and the mad waters of the lake.

For a while the gap between the boat and the shore seemed to remain the same. Then slowly it closed, and Stan saw several men appear on the dock. They were waiting to help pull in the boat and secure it.

Finally the boat rocked close to the dock. The boys tossed out the rope. The men caught it, pulled the boat in against a pair of rubber tires, and secured it. The last *puff-puff* of the motor died away as Phil turned it off.

"Thanks, guys," he said gratefully. "We'd have a real damaged boat if it weren't for you."

"We were ready to call the Coast Guard," one of the men replied, grinning.

Hardly five minutes had passed when a car drove up, stopped with a sudden jerk, and three anxious-looking people jumped out.

"Stan! Phil! Are you all right?"

The boys grinned at Mom, Dad, and Dottie, who stared at them white-faced.

"All right?" echoed Phil innocently. "Why? Is something wrong?"

Dottie's green eyes flared. "Don't be smart, Philip Andrew Martin! We saw that storm coming, and we knew you were out on the lake. You and Stan — all of you! Of course, if we knew you were such a hot-shot pilot —"

"He is!" Stan cried out seriously. "He saved our lives!"

Dottie smiled. Her eyes softened.

"I'm not so sure about that," said Phil humbly.

"Well, I am!" said Stan.

"So are we," said Larry earnestly. "If it wasn't for Phil, we might have all drowned."

"Drowned? With your life jackets on?" Phil chuckled. Even with his face streaming wet from the rain, you could see it color a little. "Look, the four of us don't mind," he went on, pointing at himself and his three companions. "But don't you folks care about getting wet?"

"Yes, we do!" Dad yelled, and led the race to the car and its shelter from the storm.

## ··· *10*

On Thursday, July 21, Stan watched the start of the Clippers-Falcons game from the bench. Some of the boys sitting beside him, especially Larry's brother Ray, Ronnie Woods, and Mose Finn, chattered without letting up a minute. They seemed satisfied just wearing the Falcons' uniform. Fuzzy Collins was more quiet, like Stan.

"Come on, you guys," said Mose. "Where's that chatter?"

This nudged Stan and Fuzzy into some yelling, but not for long.

Stan didn't know about Fuzzy, nor did he

care very much. He had his own self to worry about.

He didn't like warming the bench three or four innings a game. Of course he knew all fifteen players couldn't play at the same time, although the better ones did play every inning.

"Got to keep in the better players so no team could shellac us," Coach Bennett once said.

Not playing regularly proved he wasn't one of the better ones. That was what griped him, and made him feel the way he did now. The season was almost half over, and he wasn't a bit better now than he had been at the beginning.

Phil was right. Don't get to love the game very much. You might get awfully discouraged.

I'm awfully discouraged now, thought Stan. He watched the Clippers take their first raps and go down under Left Kellar's fast-ball pitching. The Falcons came to bat. Frankie Smith smacked a solid single, but he didn't get past first.

The Clippers started off the second inning with a single, followed by a sacrifice bunt that put the man in scoring position. A double sent him around the bases. Another run scored before the Falcons could get the Clippers out.

That last hit was a hot grounder to Gary's left side. Gary almost had it. But the ball struck the tip of his glove and went bouncing to the outfield.

*I could've caught that*, Stan thought. *I would've kept that last run from scoring.*

It looked easy from the bench.

*I have a hobby at home. My airplane and spaceship models. I can work on them. After a time I can forget baseball. A guy can forget it, can't he, if he's away from it for a while?*

By the fifth inning the Clippers had a strong

68

hold of the game. They were leading, 4 to 0.

"Okay, Stan," said Coach Bartlett. "Get on second. Lots of hustle now."

Stan picked up the new glove Dad had bought him and raced out to his position at second. A moment later the Clippers' lead-off man beat out a dribbling grounder to third. The Falcons' infield moved in, expecting a bunt.

It was a bunt! The ball rolled toward first, just inside the foul line!

George Page charged in after it. Stan rushed to cover first. At the same time Lefty ran toward first, too.

"I'll cover, Lefty!" Stan yelled.

Lefty stopped. George fielded the ball, turned, and whipped it to first. The ball just missed the runner. Stan stretched, and caught the ball in time.

"Out!" cried the umpire.

Stan felt good as he hustled back into

position. The next hitter flied out and Lefty walked the third. Then a grounder was hit to short, and Don tossed the ball to Stan at second for the forced out.

He didn't get to bat this inning, but he would the next. The Clippers, hotter than fire, mowed down the Falcons one, two, three in the bottom of the sixth, then scored two more runs at their turn at bat.

With one out and a man on, Stan stepped to the plate. He took a called strike, then leaned into a shoulder-high pitch and swung with all his might.

"Strike two!" cried the umpire, as Stan's bat swished through the empty air.

He took a ball, and then another. Now the count was two and two.

Stan stepped out of the box and touched his sweating hands into the soft dirt. *I can't strike out,* he thought. *I just can't!*

He got back into the box, and the pitcher went into his stretch. The ball breezed in.

It looked a little inside, but it might cut the corner!

Stan swung.

*Smack!*

The sound was the ball hitting the pocket of the catcher's mitt.

"You're out!" yelled the umpire.

Stan went back to the dugout, sick at heart.

Fuzzy batted for Eddie Lee, and fanned, ending the ball game. The Clippers took it, 6 to 0.

Stan spent a lot of time the next day looking at the spaceship models in the Hobby Shop on Darby Street. He would earn money somehow — there were always people who wanted their lawns cut — and save it up to buy more models. He could spend hours and hours just assembling models. It wouldn't be long before he'd forget baseball altogether.

He didn't say much around the house, but

the way everybody looked at him they certainly must have suspected that he wasn't
happy about something. Mom tried to pry
the trouble out of him, but he told her that
there was nothing wrong.

"I bet!" said Dottie, who was suspicious
about anything.

The next day he got a letter. He stared at
the address on the envelope. It was exactly
like the one he had received before. The
words were cut out of either a newspaper or
a magazine.

He tore off the end of the envelope and
took out the letter. This, too, was made up
of cut-out words.

YOU ARE GIVING UP TOO EASILY. NO BOXER
QUIT BECAUSE HE LOST A FIGHT. YOU LOVE
BASEBALL. IT'S A GOOD GAME. STICK WITH IT.

The last three words were underlined
twice in ink.

"Mom," he said, the letter trembling in

his hands, "who keeps sending me these letters?"

Mom shrugged her shoulders. "I don't know," she said. "But whoever it is must certainly know what's bothering you!"

## ··· *11*

Everybody in the family read the strange letter. If one of them had sent it, his — or her — face did not show it. Everyone acted just as surprised as Stan did, and looked at each other suspiciously, too.

Maybe it's somebody on the team, Stan thought. But who would care enough about him to send a letter like that?

Tommy Hart? Larry? Or could it be Coach Bartlett?

He did not mention the letters to any of his teammates. Maybe one of these days the person who had sent them would say something unintentionally that would give him away.

"Just the same, that letter makes good sense," Dad said. "Everybody should take its advice."

Phil's face colored a little, and he turned and walked away.

Beginning with the next practice, Stan played harder and harder. He tried to forget about himself and just do what he had to do, and do it the best he could.

He improved fast. Coach Bartlett noticed it.

"I've been noticing you, Stan," he said. "You've picked up a lot of spark lately. Just as if you've shaken off some kind of bugaboo. What's happened?"

Stan grinned shyly, and shrugged. "I don't know. Guess I'm just playing harder, that's all."

"Guess you are," said the coach. "Okay, get on second. Gary!" he shouted across the diamond. "Play short! I want to try something new!"

Gary looked puzzledly at him. "Short? But Coach, I've never played short."

"Don't say never," replied Coach Bartlett. "A good infielder plays any position in the infield. Your arm is strong. Get on short and don't argue."

Gary got on short, and Coach Bartlett began hitting grounders to him and Stan. They worked double plays. The coach showed Stan how to cover second and then throw to first when the ball was hit to short. Then he showed Gary how to work the play when the ball was hit to second.

"You're doing great," he commented after he had the boys sweating. "Something tells me you're going to turn into a great double-play combination."

Coach Bartlett said things like that. The kids liked him for it, even though what he said didn't always turn out to be true.

It was Wednesday, July 27, when the coach had Gary and Stan try out their new positions in a game. The new line-up was as follows:

| | |
|---|---|
| J. Kendall | 3b |
| S. Martin | 2b |
| F. Smith | lf |
| D. Powers | cf |
| G. Page | 1b |
| G. Newman | ss |
| L. Jones | c |
| E. Lee | rf |
| T. Hart | p |

The Falcons had first raps against the Steelers. Jim walked, and Stan laid a beautiful bunt down the first-base line to put Jim in scoring position. Frankie socked two pitches back to the screen, then whiffed. Two outs.

Duffy Powers walked to the plate and smashed the first pitch to deep center for a triple. Jim scored, and then George beat out a dribbler to third, scoring Duffy.

Gary walked, and Stan was sure that the

Steelers' coach would put in a new pitcher. But he didn't, even when Larry singled and Eddie Lee singled right behind him. It was Tommy who ended the merry-go-round, hitting a ball to deep center which the center fielder caught almost without moving.

Score: 4 to 0.

The Steelers were helpless at the plate, but for the next several innings they held the Falcons to one hit. In the fifth the Falcons found their eye again, and blasted the ball for three runs. This time the Steelers' pitcher went to the showers.

At their turn at bat, the Steelers seemed to find their eye at last. The first two batters singled, and Tommy walked the third to load the bases.

Coach Bartlett waved the infielders in.

For the first time since the game had started, Stan felt scared. What should he do if the ball was hit to him? Throw home, or to second? He looked at Gary, and then at

Tommy. But Gary was leaning forward, his hands on his knees, chattering for all he was worth. He had lots of life, Gary did. Tommy was facing third, rubbing the ball, just taking his time. He didn't look worried at all.

The first pitch was a called strike. The second was in there, too. The batter swung. *Crack!* A hot grounder down to second, right at Stan!

He had to make his decision — right *now!* Home, or first?

He caught the hop, whipped it home. Out! Larry snapped the ball to third. Safe by half a step!

"Nice peg, Stan!" said Tommy, smiling.

One away. Still three on.

A high pop fly to third, going foul, with Mose Finn going under it. Mose had taken Jim's place. A warm relief came over Stan. *Mose will catch this ball and I won't have to worry about a double play*, he thought.

The ball came down, a small, white meteor. It struck Mose's glove, and bounced out!

"Get a basket!" somebody shouted from the stands.

"Butterfingers!" Stan muttered to himself.

The next pitch was a ground ball to short. Stan raced to cover second. Gary fielded the ball and snapped it hard to Stan.

The ball struck the thumb of Stan's glove and sailed past him!

He turned, ran after the ball, and picked it up. But it was too late. A runner had just crossed the plate.

"Come on, Stan!" shouted Gary, angrily. "Hold on to 'em!"

Stan blushed. Even though it was the Steelers' first run, Stan felt that it was his fault. Gary had thrown that ball a little too hard, but he still should have had it.

Tommy fanned the next man, and the boys hustled off the field.

"You threw that ball too hard, Gary," accused Coach Bartlett. "When you're that close to second, throw it easier. Watch it the next time."

Stan looked, baffled, at the coach, and then at Gary, who went silently to the dugout. So the coach had noticed. Suddenly, he felt a lot better.

The Falcons went on to win the game, 8 to 1.

## ··· *12*

I need a vacation," said Phil just before August rolled around. "I haven't been away from home in a long time."

Dad smiled. "Where do you want to go?"

Phil shrugged. "South somewhere. Georgia. Florida. Just to see some country I haven't seen before."

Phil had no steady job. He had worked on construction for a while, on the new senior high school. Then he had had a job as a stock clerk in a computer factory. He seldom complained, but he hadn't acted satisfied with either job.

"Boy! Wish I could go with you," cried Stan.

"Maybe you can — sometime," Phil said, pinching Stan's nose. "But not this time."

"We'll miss you," Dottie said, her cheeks dimpling as she smiled. "But I think a two weeks' vacation will do you good."

Phil laughed. "Want to get rid of me?"

"Just for two weeks," replied his sister, and kissed him on the cheek.

Phil looked at Stan. "If you want any rides in the boat, little buddy, Dad will take you. Don't you ever take it out by yourself."

"Don't worry," said Stan. "Jeez, don't you think I know?"

Phil packed his suitcase, and Dad drove him to the bus station.

"Write," Dad said.

"I will," Phil promised.

Things did not go very well around second base during the practice sessions. Stan felt sure he knew what it was. Gary just didn't like the idea of Stan's taking over at second.

Was second base very different from shortstop? Stan didn't think so, yet it could be only for that reason that Gary acted that way.

Jeb was almost always at the practices, too, sitting in the dugout with his legs stretched out in front of him and his arms crossed over his chest. He had dated Dottie again and Stan didn't like that at all. There were so many real nice guys. Why did she have to go out with him?"

The funny part of it was, Stan really couldn't think of anything bad about Jeb. Maybe he just didn't *want* to like Jeb because he showed Gary pointers on the ball field. Phil never had done that with Stan.

In a way, when you thought about it, Phil was a strange sort of guy.

Gary played the entire game at short against the Red Devils. Once, a double-play ball, he threw the pill too hard to Stan just as he had done before, and Stan missed it.

The very next pitch was hit for a grounder and Stan didn't get his glove down low enough. The ball sizzled through his legs to the outfield and a run scored.

"The coach must be blind if he thinks you're an infielder," said Gary with a very angry look on his face.

A double drove in another run for the Red Devils. Stan was glad when Fuzzy Collins took his place in the fourth inning.

Two runs were all the Red Devils scored. The Falcons beat them, 5 to 2.

They trimmed the Comets, 11 to 1, and on August 4 they played the Steelers again. No team was worried about the Steelers. Whoever had named that team must have figured that they would be tough as nails. But the Steelers were in the cellar and by the looks of things would stay there.

The Falcons had a field day against them. Everybody batted around at least three times, and some four and five. Stan and Gary pulled off two sparkling double plays. Two other times Gary snapped the ball too wildly for Stan to catch. Gary said nothing at these times, as if he knew Stan couldn't possibly have caught those throws.

The Falcons had a lot of men left on. Otherwise the score would have been worse than 9 to 3.

Picture post cards came from Phil. They were stamped in Atlanta, Georgia; Memphis, Tennessee; and Nashville, Tennessee.

"Boy! He's really traveling!" murmured Stan excitedly.

Then, for a few days during the second week of Phil's vacation, there was no word from him.

"He's sent us a card almost every day," Mom said. "Guess he wants to rest a while."

But Mom looked worried. Of course there was no reason why she should be worried, but Mom was like that. Dad got a little disgusted with her.

"He's a man now, Jen. He can take care of himself. You have to get used to that fact."

"I know," Mom said quietly. "But it isn't easy."

And then, exactly on the day that was to end Phil's two weeks' vacation, Mom and Dad received a letter from him.

*Hello, everybody! Sorry I haven't dropped you even a post card these last few days, but I've been very busy. Doing what? Well, listen! I have just signed with Harport! Yes, I'm back with them, and I'm happy! I'll have to come home for some of my things, and to tell my boss I'm quitting. Until then, be good and be cheerful!*

*Love,*

*Phil*

## ··· *13*

Phil flew home and Dad drove to the airport to meet him. Stan went along, too, excited as ever over the news about Phil's playing professional baseball again.

Phil had barely climbed down the steps from the plane when Stan rushed up to him and asked:

"How are you doing, Phil? Are you hitting that apple?"

Phil grinned, and pinched Stan's nose as he sometimes did. "Maybe not like Mantle, but I'm hitting. Let's wait till I get home and I'll tell you all about it. Right now I'm so hungry I could eat a bear!"

Mom and Dottie kissed Phil as if he had

been away a year. Then Mom cooked a quick meal and everybody sat around the table listening to Phil talk while he tried to eat.

"Oh, let the poor boy eat," said Mom.

But whenever Phil said anything, she was all ears too.

"So you took your vacation just for the purpose of trying out with Harport again," said Dad, grinning.

"That's right," answered Phil between bites, his glance swinging from one to the other. "I wanted to play baseball again. Matter of fact, nobody really knows how much I missed it and wanted to play."

His eyes rested on Stan for a moment, then turned away. I know, Stan thought. I know *exactly* how he felt.

Phil said he had to return to Harport day after tomorrow. They were playing a night game.

"Oh, boy!" said Stan, and looked up at Dad

with wide, eager eyes. "Can we go back with Phil, Dad? Can we see him play?"

"That's a good idea!" said Phil. Smiling, he tapped his left hip pocket where his wallet was. "I signed for a nice bonus. The trip will be on me. Better yet, how about Mom and Dottie going, too?"

"Nothing doing!" cried Mom. "No airplane trips for me! I'm keeping my feet on the ground!"

"Mom," said Dottie, "don't be so oldfashioned. We'll make the trip. Phil will buy us all round-trip tickets, and we'll go. Right, big brother?"

"Right!" said Phil.

Mom insisted she wasn't going by air, and that was that. She kept her word, too, at least until the next afternoon.

Once again Dad got disgusted with her.

"All right," he said. "If you're not going, neither am I."

"Oh, no," Mom said. "You're going. *I'm* staying home."

When the plane departed the next afternoon, Phil, Stan, Dottie, Dad *and* Mom were on it.

Stan laughed when the plane taxied down the long runway, and then took off. Mom had her eyes closed. It wasn't until the plane was quite high that she opened them again and dared a glance out of the window.

"Oh, my," she said.

She was quiet for a while, fascinated by the view passing slowly underneath them. The earth below stretched out like a giant patchwork quilt. Hills loomed in the distance. Rivers wound crookedly, finally emptying into small lakes that flashed the sunlight like tiny mirrors.

"This is beautiful," Mom finally said. "Really beautiful."

At her side, Dad grinned with satisfaction,

winked at Stan, and then leaned his head back to rest.

The game, played under lights, drew a large crowd. Stan and his family sat in reserved seats, directly behind the Harport dugout. Phil, dressed in his white uniform, winked at them as he walked past. Broad-shouldered and head held high, he looked even taller than he did in regular clothes.

The game got under way. Phil played short, and Stan watched him eagerly. It had been a long time since he had seen Phil play. Phil moved lightly on his feet, and he threw the ball like a bullet.

Each time a ball galloped down to short, Stan bit his lip. But Phil played the ball like the professional he was, catching the hop and whipping it to first for the put-out. Once he worked a double play without an assist. The ball was hit to his side of second base. Running hard, he nabbed the ball in his gloved hand, stepped on the bag, then pegged to first.

Then, in the fifth inning, he fumbled a hard-hit grounder. He finally picked up the ball and fired it to first, but the runner was already there.

"Oh-oh," muttered Dad.

Stan got nervous. How would Phil act now? Would that error bother him so that he might miss another? Or would he not play as well as he had been playing the earlier part of the game?

In the seventh inning a hard-driven ball headed between third and short. There were two outs, and a man was on third. Harport trailed by one run. This extra run would be an "insurance" run for the other team.

Phil's too far from it! thought Stan. He just can't possibly get that ball!

Then Phil stretched out his *bare right hand,* caught the ball, and pegged it to first!

The throw was long, swift, and accurate. It beat the runner by a step!

"Wow!" gasped Dad. "Did you see that?"

"Man, what a catch!" cried Stan.

The fans gave Phil a big hand.

So far, at the plate, Phil had grounded out and drawn a walk. Now, with a man on, he stepped into the batter's box again. He was a right-hand hitter. He stood tall and loose.

The pitches came in, and he looked them over carefully. At last he had a full count on him — three and two.

"This is the one that counts," whispered Stan excitedly.

The pitch came in, and Phil smacked it. It sailed far out to left, over the fielder's head! The ball struck the fence and bounced back. A run scored and Phil stopped on third base with a triple.

The next hitter scored Phil. Harport kept ahead the rest of the game and won it, 4 to 3.

The crowd cheered, and then began to drift out of the ball park.

Dad stood up, a pleased smile on his lips.

"Phil will stay with the game now," he said, almost to himself. "He's not afraid of losing any more. He's not afraid of making errors, or striking out. I wonder what made him change his mind?"

## ··· *14*

The family stayed at a motel that night. They saw Phil the next morning for a while, and both Dad and Stan praised him.

"Man, what a catch you made!" said Stan. "Didn't that ball sting?"

Phil grinned. "A little."

They spent a couple of hours with him, seeing some of the sights around the city. Then they had lunch with him. Later a taxi drove them to the airport, and they boarded their plane for home.

Stan watched clouds drift past the right wing of the big plane.

"I've been thinking about Phil, Dad," he said.

"You have?"

"Yes. I bet he's thought about those letters. Those mysterious letters I've been getting. What do you think, Dad?"

His father patted his knee and smiled. "I wouldn't be a bit surprised, son. Not surprised at all."

After the plane landed, Dad called a taxi to drive them home.

When Stan walked into his room, he found a package on his bed. It was box-shaped, and wrapped in red and white striped paper with a large bow. Stan looked for a tag but didn't find it.

"It *must* be mine," he said to himself, his heart tingling.

He took off the bow and the wrapping. The box clearly showed what the package contained. A *Voyager* model!

"Phil gave it to me!" he shouted.

Sure enough, there was a card inside the

box. *Hi, little buddy. I hope you like this. Phil.*

Stan carried it out to the living room, almost stumbling in his haste, and showed it to Mom, Dad, and Dottie. They acted surprised, but almost immediately he knew they were only pretending. They had known about the package all the time!

He spent the next morning putting the model together. In the afternoon he looked over the baseball schedule and discovered that the Falcons had a game with the Jaguars. They had split with the Jags before, so Stan wasn't worried.

Suddenly he remembered Gary whipping the ball to him so hard that he had to miss it. How could Coach Barrett expect to make a good combination around second base if Gary insisted on being bullheaded?

Mom, Dad, and Dottie came to the game and sat in the bleachers behind first base.

Stan wished they hadn't come. He and Gary were starting, and he knew that things weren't going to go just right between them.

Then he remembered the letters, and Phil. Phil had conquered the thing that had held him back from playing baseball. It must have been the letters — those strange, mysterious letters — that had changed Phil.

*As long as I think about those letters I feel all right. It's as though they have some magic power.*

The Jaguars were first up. A pop fly and two grounders to the infield took care of their first three men.

Jim Kendall, leading off for the Falcons, drew a walk, and Stan bunted him to second.

Frankie Smith, digging in hard, hit a dribbler down to second. He was thrown out, but Jim advanced to third. Then Duffy got up and lifted a high fly toward left field. It soared like a meteor. This ball was really going into orbit. Duffy tossed his bat aside and beat it for first.

But then the ball curved, and disappeared over the left-field fence!

"Foul ball!" boomed the umpire.

Duffy was nearly to second base. Shaking his head, he cut back across the diamond, picked up his bat, and tried it again. The Jaguars' pitcher slipped the next one by him. Then Duffy poled one to center field and the ball was caught.

Three away.

The Jaguars' clean-up man swung two bats from one shoulder to the other as he stood just outside the batter's box. Then he flipped one aside and stepped to the plate. He was a left-hand hitter and looked mighty dangerous.

The outfielders moved toward the right. Eddie Lee went back ten steps. In the field Stan and George Page backed to the edge of the grass.

Tommy got his signal, wound up, and delivered.

"Ball one!" shouted the umpire.

The next one was in there, and the batter swung. *Crack!* A high fly ball over second base!

Stan ran back for it, watching the ball constantly. Ahead of him he heard Eddie Lee coming toward him on a mad run, and a horrible fright went through him. He'd read about players colliding. Sometimes it resulted in a serious injury. That mustn't happen now! Not when he had a chance to nab that fly!

"Let me take it, Eddie!" he yelled desperately. "Let me take it!"

"Go ahead!" cried Eddie.

The ball came down swiftly over his left shoulder. Stan put out his glove. *Smack!* He had it!

"Nice catch, Stan!" said Eddie.

Cheers and loud applause greeted Stan as

he turned and pegged the ball in to Gary. A warm feeling overwhelmed him as he trotted back to his position. He noticed that Gary didn't say a word, but Stan didn't care now.

I'll play the best I can. I'll hustle after every ball. If I make an error I won't feel as if the world has dropped on my head. Even major leaguers miss them sometimes. I'll try not to worry, or get disgusted again. Those are the things I must remember. And if I must sit on the bench, so what? There's another day coming, and another game.

Tommy fanned the next batter, and the third batter popped out.

"Let's pick up some runs," urged Coach Bartlett as the Falcons came to bat.

But the innings slipped by, and they didn't get a man on base. That little right-hander on the mound for the Jaguars was pitching a great game. Frankie, Duffy, Stan, and a couple of others had gone down swinging at his fast ball.

"What's he got? Nothing!" grumbled Duffy. Yet the little pitcher had the Falcons eating out of his hand.

And then, in the fifth, with none on, the Jaguars' clean-up hitter broke the nothing-nothing tie. He poled one over the left-field fence for a home run.

# ··· *15*

The long hit inspired the Jaguars. The next man singled. Then, even though Jim and George played in on the grass, a bunt got by Jim, and men were safe on first and second.

The Falcons' infield began to chatter seriously. Coach Bartlett had put substitutes in several positions, but still kept in Gary and Stan.

Then — a hard-hit ball down to short! Gary fielded it, pegged it to Stan!

A wild throw! It sailed past Stan, and the runners moved! Fuzzy Collins, now playing first, chased after the ball. The runners reached their bases and held up.

Bases loaded and no outs!

The infielders moved in. The Jaguars had one run, but a hit now could mean one or two more. Possibly three. It would be a shame to let the Jaguars plaster them with a shutout like that.

Tommy Hart worked hard on the batter and struck him out. Then a ground ball was hit to second, only a few feet from the bag. Stan raced for it and caught it in his gloved hand. He could touch the bag and throw to first. Or he could touch the runner coming from first and then throw it. But he might lose some precious time. He didn't dare risk it.

He tossed the ball easily and accurately to Gary. Gary stepped on the edge of the bag, then pegged the ball to first.

A double play!

Three outs, and the Falcons trotted in, glad that that hectic inning was over.

Coach Bartlett motioned to Gary. Stan,

sitting within earshot of them, heard the coach say:

"Gary, you had better change your attitude out there or I'll have to bench you the next game, our last of the season. I've warned you once before. I won't again. Knock that chip off your shoulder and play ball as you should. Don't think for one minute I haven't noticed how you've been acting toward Stan. I thought I was doing you a favor by putting you at short. Shortstop's about the toughest position on the diamond. You can field grounders well, and throw well. You could have thrown that ball to Stan for a double play easily, but you deliberately threw it hard and wild. You didn't make him look bad. You made yourself look bad."

Gary's face turned red, and he looked toward the end of the dugout. Jeb was sitting there, gazing out upon the field.

"Don't look at Jeb for sympathy," said the coach. "It's time you thought things out for yourself. Okay. That's all. But remember what I said. Get on deck. You're second batter."

Stan couldn't believe his ears. He realized he was staring and his mouth was open. He caught Larry looking at him, and blushed. Larry winked.

The Falcons failed to score at all, and the game went to the Jaguars, 1 to 0. It was still a shutout, but a very good game.

The Falcons closed the season on Friday against the Comets, who carried home the victory 8 to 2. Gary played. He and Stan worked a double play, and afterwards he flashed a grin to Stan to prove that the chip on his shoulder was gone forever.

The next day the *Courier-Star* printed the League standings.

| Teams | Won | Lost | Games Behind |
|-------|-----|------|--------------|
| Jaguars | 11 | 4 | — |
| Clippers | 10 | 5 | 1 |
| Falcons | 8 | 7 | 3 |

| Comets | 7 | 8 | 4 |
| Red Devils | 6 | 9 | 5 |
| Steelers | 3 | 12 | 8 |

"Well, we didn't do so bad. Did we, Dad?" said Stan.

Dad smiled. "Not at all. By the way, you received a letter in the mail."

He was holding it in his hand. Stan shivered as he saw the familiar printing on the envelope.

"Another one?" he cried.

He opened it with eager, trembling fingers. Then he pulled out the letter and read it.

CONGRATULATIONS! WE THINK YOU'VE LICKED IT. AND SO HAS PHIL. YOUR EVER-LOVING FANS, DOTTIE AND JEB.

Stan's eyes widened. "Dottie and Jeb?" he shouted.

Dad laughed. "That's right. They've been the writers of those mysterious letters."

Stan was flabbergasted. Then he chuckled. "Got any old newspapers, Dad?" he asked. "I'm going to answer that letter!"